Haiku Horror Stories

by Carey Burns

Haiku Horror Stories

By Carey Burns

ISBN-13: 978-0615715971
ISBN-10: 0615715974

Front cover art by Jill Hejl

About this book

Haiku is a Japanese form of poetry. A haiku has three lines with five syllables in the first, seven syllables in the second, and five syllables in the third. Traditional haikus have a specific subject matter, but my haikus are not traditional. Here is an example of one of my haikus:

Once the howling stops
Is when you should really run
They can taste your fear

I have enjoyed writing haikus since grade school (which is many, many years ago) and recently began to twist them into micro flash fiction stories with rather dark subject matter.

This is a collection of my favorite haiku horror stories with a handful of individual haikus mixed in for good measure. I hope you enjoy reading them.

When the cold wind blows
And the moon is overhead
I believe in ghosts

Toy Collector

Down the dusty streets
The cart rattled to a stop
And the driver sighed

He pulled off his cap
And hopped down from his high seat
Then rang a brass bell

One by one, mothers
Came out to his small wagon
Clutching worn out toys

They stood in a line
For a moment to bargain
With the ancient man

He might take the toys
To help bring back their loved ones
Or he might say no

He judged each child's worth
By the wear on the old toys
None were worn enough

But then a woman
Handed him an old troll doll
Filthy and broken

He held the sad toy
And placed it in the wagon
Then rang the bell once

As he drove away
All the mothers departed
Except for the last

She stood in the street
And saw her Carolina
Come back from the dead

I heard the child cry
"Please, why won't someone help me?"
As wolves howled with glee

Giant Feast

Across the mountains
Lives a large tribe of giants
Who eat small children

Once ev'ry summer
They raid our small villages
Stealing our young ones

They roast them in pits
For their elaborate feasts
'Til they're golden brown

This year they'll be shocked
To find them full of poison
And then they will die

Then come next summer
We'll have elaborate feasts
Of game big and small

He reeked of sour sweat
And layers of nicotine
Stained his teeth yellow

Free

Duct tape tears my lips
As I pull it from my mouth
With one quick motion

He doesn't know it
But I untied my bound hands
And I am now free

I creep to the door
And then waver a moment
Afraid to escape

What if he hears me?
Can I even outrun him?
Will he shoot me dead?

I take a deep breath
Throw open the door and run
Like Hell for the road

No one could find her
But they should have looked harder
And now it's too late

Out of Body

I see my blood pool
Under my torso and head
Then float up higher

My eyes stare at me
Surprised that I am dying
Like that all alone

I float to the path
That leads up to the playground
And I see him there

He just walks away
Like he has no idea
I even exist

Flies swarm at the wound
Seeking a home for their young
It's death's nursery

Jane Doe

I'm dead in a ditch
Like you always have worried
Sorry it came true

The tattoos I got
Joking that they'd ID me
Are only skin deep

Bones are what remain
Of my once living body
That now is a corpse

Maybe they'll find me
When they mow in the springtime
Another Jane Doe

Blood on the ceiling
From a fine misty spraying
Of jugular blood

The Hunter

The fiend comes at night
Waiting in dark shadowed streets
Until he sees her

Blood lust drives him to
Follow her home and sneak in
While she drifts to sleep

Fangs pierce her soft flesh
And he gorges on her blood
Until she is cold

Then he sneaks away
Under cover of darkness
'Til tomorrow night

I danced on your grave
But then I screamed like a girl
When you grabbed my leg

The Canoe Trip

We pulled up to shore
And I spied the pentagram
Made out of deer bones

I wanted to leave
But nobody would listen
They beached the canoe

I stayed in the boat
While they kicked at the symbol
Knocking over bones

I grabbed at an oar
And pushed off in the current
Leaving them stranded

I still hear their cries
As I paddle the river
But I can't go back

I hope you'll forget
How she looked when you found her
And how your heart ached

Aliens

The cow lay there dead
Its face stripped down to the bone
Its gut ripped open

The farmer was scared
He feared it was a message
Sent from the spacemen

The very next night
He stood watch with a shotgun
In case they returned

Round about midnight
He saw something creep closer
To his herd of cows

He shot and it fell
So he ran to his victim
The neighbor boy Bill

I was left behind
And they said they'd come for me
One just broke the door

Lost Tooth

I chewed my sandwich
And bit down on a loose tooth
But it wasn't mine

I dropped it and screamed
And my lunch mates grew quiet
When they saw the tooth

"Where did it come from?"
They asked in disgusted tones
While I rinsed my mouth

"I made it myself
It's just leftover chicken
I shredded last night."

"It has a filling."
Said one of the braver girls
"You sure it's not yours?"

I wriggled my tongue
Over my teeth "Nope. All there."
Where did it come from?

Lunch was then over
All of our appetites lost
Because of a tooth

Cold breeze tickles skin
And I feel someone watching
Why does he haunt me?

Timber

There's a tree outside
With a face like a demon
I do not trust it

Sometimes it grins wide
As if it has a secret
That it wants to tell

Other times it sneers
Like it's plotting out my death
And biding its time

Often, in moonlight
It grimaces with great pain
From some fatal wound

But after today
It won't bother me again
I have a new saw

Black and white photo
Of grandma's great-grandmother
And I have her eyes

Death to Tradition

Black crows and stray dogs
Pick through the bones in delight
Until something falls

The wooden platform
Shades the greasy dirt below
And the dogs return

Above bodies rot
Far from their loved ones' warm homes
Until bones are clean

I pick up the skulls
And return to my chamber
I'm greeted by friends

Grinning skulls in rows
Painted by my hand with care
No two are alike

My work is unclean
And I am an old woman
Who will paint my skull?

The bare branches sway
Casting shadows on the wall
But shadows don't laugh

Afraid of the Dark

I woke with a start
Something sniffed at my window
And now it is gone

I pull up my sheet
As if it could protect me
From what is outside

My heart shakes my chest
As I try to be quiet
So it can't hear me

I breathe so shallow
That I start to feel dizzy
And even more scared

There it is again
Only now it is louder
It rattles the sash

The window opens
And I squeeze my eyes closed tight
Willing it to leave

Then I hear it laugh
And I let out a whisper
Just before it strikes

The bloated corpse rose
And floated to the surface
His crime now exposed

Sink or Swim

She jumped from the dock
With such youthful abandon
A smile on her face

She splashed me and laughed
Coaxed me into the water
I smiled but stayed put

Soon she grew sluggish
And struggled with her drugged arms
Trying to reach shore

Eyes open, she sank
Way down under the water
Coherent but numb

She didn't react
When she saw the girl's body
Trapped under the dock

Warm breath on my neck
Breath held, I turn around slow
There's nobody there

Hot Date

I paint on red lips
Right in front of the mirror
And get that odd sense

Like I'm not alone
But I look in the mirror
And there's no one there

It must be my nerves
Tonight is our second date
And I hope it's good

Before I can turn
Unseen, cruel fangs pierce my neck
My blood flows, I swoon

Life leaves my body
And my eyes flutter to see
His smiling red lips

Fog snakes through the trees
I run, tripping on my skirt
Just like the movies

The Stranger

They dragged the river
But never found her body
And they were so close

Just off the main path
That leads down to the boat launch
That's where she's buried

The soil was sandy
And the digging was easy
Besides, she was small

She looked so peaceful
As I covered her with dirt
Like she was sleeping

But her bloodied lip
And the rope around her neck
Hinted she was dead

Over ten years passed
And it's like I just left her
Buried on the bank

They'll never find her
Only I know where she is
And I'm a stranger

No signs of life as
Feet slip-slop through clotting blood
It was a bloodbath

Elves and the Shoemaker

The shoemaker sighed
Broken, torn and tattered shoes
Cluttered his work bench

He closed his eyes tight
Wishing the elves would come back
And help him once more

He lay down to sleep
Sure they'd come just like before
While he was sleeping

They did indeed come
Spiteful that he took credit
For all their hard work

They destroyed the shoes
That he had worked so hard on
Then they broke his tools

And with leather cord
They strangled the shoemaker
Until he was dead

We bury the dead
(After preserving their flesh)
In airtight caskets

Honeycomb

It started with one
A single bee in the house
And then more bees came

They found a small crack
High up on the plaster wall
And settled inside

The walls hummed loudly
As they built up their sweet hive
Safe in the old house

When a man moved in
And claimed the house for his own
The bees didn't mind

Then he smashed the wall
With a heavy sledgehammer
Shattering plaster

Alarm swept the hive
And hundreds emerged to fight
All willing to die

He heard the wall hum
Then felt their stings all over
And screamed in great pain

Bees swarmed in his mouth
And honey dripped down the wall
As he collapsed, dead

I cannot see how
The macramé plant holder
Swayed without a breeze

Phone Call

The moving fan blades
Stutter the light as she waits
For the phone to ring

"I'll call you" he said
"To let you know if it's safe"
That was days ago

She thinks they got him
Tore at his flesh with their teeth
Until he was dead

She hopes that he's safe
That he won't rise from the dead
And seek out her flesh

The phone trills just once
And she lifts it to her ear
But the line goes dead

The cats keep growling
Hissing, glaring at the wall
But there's nothing there

Mail Call

I opened the lid
And saw the dead bird inside
Its blood on my mail

First it was a mouse
Still in the spring-loaded trap
Left there to scare me

Next a rabbit's leg
Severed from some poor creature
Just to torture me

There's always something
Left for me by the postman
I'll tip him next year

Never wear high heels
They make it harder to run
Away from zombies

Encounter

Bright lights lit the sky
But not like from an airplane
Or helicopter

They were different
Had a strange unearthly glow
That didn't seem right

I watched them hover
Above me in the backyard
As if scanning me

I felt my flesh burn
Where a white-hot beam focused
On my exposed arm

When I cried in pain
The lights moved away in haste
'Til they streaked the sky

The burn has festered
Oozing out rank pus and blood
Through the fresh bandage

I need a doctor
But if I tell what happened
He'll think that I'm nuts

The stink makes me gag
I didn't ever want you
To end up this way

Strange New World

Zombies brought the flies
And the flies brought the maggots
Which became more flies

Spiders multiplied
With the overabundance
Just like the frogs did

It's a strange new world
Where zombies, spiders, and frogs
Outnumber humans

The door creaks open
"Is somebody there?" I ask
All's quiet and dark

Rats

The scratching has stopped
But now that worries me more
Since I can't hear them

With flashlight in hand
I set out for the kitchen
To investigate

It's just as I feared
The rats have gnawed through the wall
And are loose inside

One Mississippi
Was counted ages ago
Dare I call for help?

Déjà vu

And my hands tremble
As I see his flannel shirt
I've dreamed this before

He has the same scowl
And he stares into my eyes
Like he's dreamed me too

I beg you to leave
That something bad is coming
You can see my fear

So we turn and leave
Safe from his murderous rage
I saw in my dream

Rivulets of sand
Rain down upon my body
The casket won't hold

Female Trouble

I just bite my lip
As the blood streams down my leg
Something isn't right

Anemic and weak
I listen to the doctors
Living with the pain

No need to worry
It's just a benign tumor
No need for concern

Ultrasound...CT
Both show the same thing—fibroid
Surgery next week

Five inch incision
And something unexpected
Eyes...nose...hair and teeth

No one ever said
Infanticide was easy
But when you're in Rome...

Let Him Go

I said I love you
As I saw you gasp for air
Your eyes watering

Just before you died
With tubes and wires, you lay there
Sucking air in pain

Eyes closed, I see you
How do we choose if you live
Or just let you go?

Quality of life
Or brain-dead and not living,
How can we decide?

Love said let you go
And it's a burden we bear
With pain in our hearts

Slip-slide down the chute
Slop-splat in a steaming heap
It's worse than offal

Vultures

Greasy wings spread wide
They embrace the morning sun
Nature's housekeepers

No gristle too tough
Nor rotten stench too horrid
For their snapping beaks

But watch as they soar
Searching and circling for food
You'll see their beauty

Down in the rushes
Grubby sluggy wormthing waits
His hands slither quick

Cephalopod Dreams

In distant heavens
He lies sleeping, so they say
He's closer than that

In jet black waters
He floats out-of-time, alone
Waiting for the day

And He'll rise above
Curled tentacles unfurling
As he greets the day

Will you be ready?
Will you welcome the Old Ones
Or die with the rest?

Someday I will die
Sprinkle my ashes on Poe
And at St. Joseph

Forget Me Not

Paperbacks cram shelves
Along hardbacks stacked with care
Orphaned and alone

She was prolific
Churning out tale after tale
Like she was on fire

Gray streaks in her hair
And dementia claimed her mind
Arthritis, her hands

She stares at the spines
Wondering where they came frcm
Why they say her name

And they'll remind her
"You wrote all of those books, ma'am"
But she won't recall

How many humans
Does a spider eat each year
While it is sleeping?

Bug Bites

It started so small
A red mark from some bug bite
Didn't even itch

It grew bit by bit
A goose egg behind my ear
Tender to the touch

Just an infection
Took some antibiotics
And warm compresses

Perfect conditions
For them to grow and mature
Just under my skin

The night of their birth
I lay fevered and crying
For the pain to stop

The pain did stop, yes
Much to my horror and shock
As my skin split wide

Blood streamed down my neck
And they squiggled in the red
Unnatural birth

The bus pulled away
And the cat dragged itself free
With its two good legs

Last One Left Cleans Up the Mess

I woke up alone
And I wondered where he went
So I searched the house

The house was empty
And the car was in the drive
The cat was asleep

So I went outside
And walked around for a bit
Still in my nightgown

Nobody was out
Strange, for a beautiful day
And I went back home

I called up my mom
But her phone just rang and rang
Where could she have gone?

It's been three months now
And it really worries me
That I'm all alone

I've spent all my days
Freeing pets trapped in their homes
So that they won't starve

She was murdered here
And her specter haunts the halls
She is not at rest

Pull the Covers Over Your Head

The big black shadow
Swirling just above my bed
Still terrifies me

It has followed me
Since I was a little girl
Everywhere I go

Sometimes it comes close
And I feel it's cold, dank air
Creep over my skin

Most of the time, though
It hovers over my feet
Floating down then up

Blankets protect me
So I cover head to toe
Sometimes I can't breathe

If it touches me
It might take my soul, or worse
Do nothing at all

"He kept to himself"
The neighbors said on the news
What about the smell?

That Ain't All He Killed

There's human remains
Stuffing the freezer and fridge
The tub is stained red

Parts of twenty men
Lay scattered on the counter
And flies buzz and swarm

Such horrors they find
Makes their stomachs churn and spew
For the evening news

Serial killers
They look just like you and me
Could be right next door

Now we carry mace
And suspect all the neighbors
As they suspect us

We are all victims
When we lose security
In our own damn homes

I say it 'thoo loo'
But you say it's 'kuh thoo loo'
We'll die either way

In the Dark Water

Some dreams are so real
Even now I think them true
Awake and sober

The whispered voices
That hum in the background noise
Come clearer, sharper

Standing on the shore
I'm called to join them beyond
In the dark water

I've been here before
In dreams I've walked this foul shore
Something tells me 'Run!'

Before I dive in
Clarity embraces me
And I run like Hell

Know this when you go
Morticians know your secrets
Nothing you can hide

One Stop Shop

I sew your lips shut
To stop your pitiful cries
From piercing my ears

I sew your eyes closed
So you can't see what I do
With the rest of you

I pierce your organs
In and out with the trocar
And feel your flesh writhe

Now you lay trembling
As I insert the needle
To finish my work

Embalming alive
Makes the whole process quicker
I'm a one stop shop

The plastic bag squished
Against the toe of my shoe
Kissing it with red

Going Green

The corn was knee-high
And the rows stretched out a mile
Green bands on black dirt

Cars that passed on by
Just saw a simple cornfield
Along the highway

An unspoken bond
Between me and the farmer
For many a year

There's bodies out there
Rotting away in the rows
Severed with great care

They nourish the soil
While hidden from prying eyes
Until harvest time

He'll collect the bones
And grind them in his grain mill
For fertilizer

Our system suits us
And I see no need to change
What we have going

I hunt them for him
And delivery is free
He takes it from there

You just never know
The monsters locked in their hearts
Until they show you

Grandma's Attic

More flies day by day
I think I've killed two dozen
Just today alone

The windows are shut
And the cracks have all been sealed
Where do they come from?

With flashlight in hand
I pull down the attic stairs
And more flies swarm me

The air is thick, warm
And something smells not quite right
As I climb each tread

At the top I stop
Flashlight beam shining ahead
And I hear their drone

Thousands of black flies
Glisten on the attic floor
Writhing in a mass

I squint, crouching low
Coaxed by a curled up finger
On the floor below

I stand, turn, and walk
Down the dusty, wooden steps
Away from the hand

I push the stairs up
Trying hard to be quiet
So she won't hear me

This is Grandma's house
And she hates to be woken
When she is napping

Hurricane Party
Ended with poor Margaret
Impaled by a pole

When the Lights Go Out

The winds beat the door
And the lights cast me in black
As the power fails

Feeling my way slow
I make it to the window
But there is no light

Maybe a down line
Or something struck by lightning
No cause for alarm

Then I see him there
Staring at me from the street
Drenched from head to toe

Fear clutches my heart
Fight or flight instinct ignites
And I bolt the door

Crouched low, I scramble
Blindly into the kitchen
Searching for a knife

I sit on the floor
Panting as I listen hard
For movement outside

Time passes slowly
As the adrenaline fades
And I feel silly

I find out later
That my neighbor was murdered
Just moments before

Eight eyes and eight legs
That's nice, but I still see you
Lurking over there

Predators

Deep in the jungle
In the hot and heavy mists
Are beasts of legends

Fantastic beings
So enormous they blend in
With the canopy

Take care where you tread
Vibrations cause them alarm
They are quick to move

One step they have you
They hold you close in their arms
You won't take step two

Their fangs pierce your skin
As they pull you up the trunks
To their gauzy homes

It was just a toy
But we conjured up demons
From the pits of Hell

My Own Amityville

It's 3:33
And I hear the same strange noise
I've heard for a month

It always wakes me
At this horrible dark hour
And terrifies me

I check through the house
But nobody is lurking
In the dark shadows

There are no rodents
The house isn't settling
And I don't have pets

The air feels heavy
I leave my bedroom light on
But still I hear it

The stone in my hand
Sparkled like it was aflame
The demon was near

Unfriendly Spirit

Such strange things happened
From the moment we moved in
To that quaint white house

Cold spots in the hall
And disembodied voices
Should have been a clue

Things moved on their own
And our cat was tormented
By something unseen

Then it turned on me
Throwing razors at me twice
While I washed my hair

Once it grabbed my leg
As I climbed the basement steps
And I bruised my knee

An old man, we're told,
Fell down those steps while canning
And died in the house

Is it his spirit
That wants us to leave his house
Or something much worse?

This night still thrills me
And I walk a bit faster
Through the fallen leaves

Haunted House

A big haunted house
It was supposed to be fun
Just a little scare

We went as a group
And I was the last in line
Behind my best friend

We screamed and we laughed
At the bright lights and noises
As we walked on through

Then, amid strobe lights
I was grabbed and dragged away
Through a hidden door

My screams don't matter
They just seem part of the act
And I can't get out

I beat on the walls
And stumble in the darkness
Falling to my knees

I feel something wet
And smell something coppery
Then reach out my hand

I think it's a man
He's not moving, but still warm
His skull is crushed in

I sit beside him
Crying, not sure what to do
And I have to pee

How many like me
Are unwilling actors here
Trapped inside the walls?

Monsters on display
In glass cases come to life
When the patrons leave

Nine Leaves

You cursed ancient soul
Trapped within strips of linen
Wonder of tana

I brew leaves for you
Yet you lay cold, unmoving
In spite of the spells

Will you awaken
And destroy my enemies
Or meet with the pyre?

I add one more leaf
Just as you reach out your hand
And strangle me dead

Footprints in the snow
And an inhuman howling
Proof that Bigfoot walks

Danger in the Woods

The glass exploded
As a deer crashed the windows
In the living room

It dashed down the hall
And left a trail of crimson
And mud in its wake

I sat there in shock
From the noise, mess, and blood stains
All in an instant

Out on the front porch
A shadowy figure stood
It was not human

It followed its prey
And I ducked behind the couch
Skin tingling in fright

With a roar it ran
Following the fresh blood trail
And I held my breath

I heard the deer cry
As the beast tore it to shreds
Further in the house

When I cough up phlegm
I try hard not to swallow
Might be a hookworm

Souvenirs

There it was again
Making his vision swimmy
But then it was gone

He lay down to rest
With a dull ache in his eye
And soon was dozing

Then a jolt of pain
Rocked his body and he woke
Covering his eye

Something wasn't right
It felt like his eye would pop
From all the pressure

He stood and staggered
The pain causing vertigo
As tears streaked his cheeks

He turned on the light
And screamed at his reflection
That stared out from the mirror

He gazed at his eye
Horrified by the creature
Wiggling from inside

With stupid courage
He grabbed a pair of tweezers
And pulled on the beast

Inch by inch it slid
Tearing his eye with each pull
Until it was free

It writhed and twisted
Against the metal pincers
As his hand trembled

He rinsed out a glass
And dropped the foul worm inside
Then called nine-one-one

It tried to get out
So he sealed it in cling wrap
And it surrendered

He lay on the floor
His eye oozing and swollen
And throbbing with pain

In a dazed stupor
He remembered Africa
When he was a boy

He lived there for years
But all he had was pictures
And this souvenir

Zombie Queen

She knows your bald soul
And she'll keep your secrets safe
But it will cost you

To the world you're dead
But by night you do her will
Powerless to stop

Your grave is empty
And her magic spurs you on
Restless shambling lost

You gather more souls
More secrets for her to keep
More zombies to rule

The ground quaked and shook
And I saw the ceiling split
Trapped in the cellar

The Creatures from the Lock

I walked the canal
Racing against the sunset
That's when they come out

Stories of huge beasts
With rat-like teeth and sharp claws
Hairless, foul, and pale

They hunt in small packs
And block your path east and west
So that you are trapped

Canal to the north
With dense forest to the south
I pick up my pace

As I near the bridge
I can see the parking lot
My calves are on fire

I hear soft growling
And see movement up ahead
I skid to a stop

Three sets of green eyes
Flash at me in the darkness
I pray they are dogs

And closer they creep
As tall as German Shepherds
With ratty faces

Their jaws snap at me
And I close my eyes real tight
Before they attack

The deadly toxins
Paralyzed me head to toe
I can still feel pain

Why Humboldt Squid Scare Me

The first squid attacked
Luminous in the water
Flashes of color

They screamed with each bite
Certain the devil had them
And this was their Hell

More squid saw the fight
And finished off the couple
A feeding frenzy

More flashing colors
A signal of rage or food
Only the squid know

Full, they swam away
While an empty boat floated
In the calm waters

The world is too wide
And too full of mysteries
We haven't found yet

The Devil's Triangle

The radio died
And the captain shook his head
Lost on the ocean

Their short pleasure cruise
Went south when the gauges froze
And the compass spun

With no direction
And no way to call for help
He looked to the skies

They had sailed into
The Bermuda Triangle
Without knowing it

Low on food and gas
They couldn't even catch a fish
But the bar was stocked

After three hot days
And their constant bickering
He couldn't take it

He stared at their flab
Hunger wipes out all taboos
And he was hungry

Long bony fingers
Point at me in the darkness
They will make me pay

Is This Hell?

The ground split in two
And the chasm yawned twelve feet
It was deep and dark

I studied it hard
Why I climbed down, I don't know
I just needed to

I picked my way down
As soil rained on my head
From the ground shifting

I couldn't see light
But the layers of rock glowed
To guide my descent

I climbed further down
And found a gaping cavern
So I crept inside

I stumbled through, blind
And froze when I heard a voice
In a foreign tongue

A faint orange glow
Tempted me in the darkness
And I crept closer

I saw a large fire
Ringed by three unearthly beasts
Sitting on boulders

Stalactites hid me
While I watched them eat their feast
Bones littered the ground

Near my foot, a skull
Grinned at me with hollow orbs
Telling me to run

I made my way back
Quiet as a mouse and quick
Fear prodding my heels

And lord, how I climbed
Fingernails bleeding and split
Grime layered my skin

I sprinted for help
Dragging Father from his chores
To see the Hell Gap

I told what I saw
And pointed him to the spot
Too afraid to go

I saw him look down
And turn around back to me
"There's nothing here, child"

Walking Ghost Tours

I showed up at nine
At the cemetery gates
Like the ad told me

We were a small group
Five of us total, strangers
All history buffs

Our guide came promptly
Dressed in a black suit and tie
Holding a lantern

We followed down rows
Enraptured by his sad tales
Of those underground

We came to a crypt
And he led us all inside
To read inscriptions

I studied the names
And froze when I heard laughter
And squeals from the door

The group stood outside
Grinning beyond the threshold
They shut the crypt door

Alone in the dark
I prayed they were just joking
That it was a test

The crypt fooled my mind
Shadows danced and I heard things
Was I not alone?

A cold hand touched me
And I screamed and beat the door
Still, fangs pierced my throat

Makeup smeared from tears
Stuttering breaths choking me
Scared to cry for help

Just Another Myth

The first rays of dawn
Kissed his skin but he just laughed
Just another myth

Like garlic, useless
And they do cast reflections
Crosses don't repel

But a wooden stake
Or decapitation does
Though they are crafty

They walk among us
Laughing at our ignorance
And peasant beliefs

Just one clumsy move
And I cut off my finger
That's what I'll tell them

Family Heirlooms

I found a wolf skin
In grandpa's old steamer trunk
With his old war stuff

Ratty and dusty
I stroked the coarse fur and smiled
Did he kill this wolf?

Draped round my shoulders
It hung down long past my waist
And was so heavy

First I felt queasy
Then I broke out in a sweat
I ached in my bones

I stared at my arm
The wolf skin and mine were joined
My hands became paws

I fell to the floor
My body shifting, changing
Into something else

Then I was the wolf
Frothing, growling, hungry beast
Frantic for the hunt

I sniffed at the air
And knew food was close at hand
Grandma was sleeping

The campground seemed safe
'Til Jenny found the bleached skull
Next to our campsite

A Day at the Fair

Round and round it goes
The chair rocks with our movement
Squeaking and groaning

As we reach the top
You plant a kiss on my cheek
And I hold your hand

The Ferris wheel stops
So I nuzzle your shoulder
Afraid to look down

Sparks fly and a crash
As neon lights hit the ground
I hear screams below

The carnie just smiles
His cigarette in his mouth
Drooping from his lip

I squeeze your hand hard
Waiting for the ride to move
But we're just stuck there

I feel metal groan
And the whole thing starts to sway
Like it is dancing

Something snaps nearby
Our chair dangles by a bolt
And we hold on tight

Screams from the riders
Sound distant as I focus
Just hold on, hold on

My hands start to slip
And I whimper, so afraid
But you can't reach me

And in slow motion
My fingers ease their death grip
And I fall, fall, fall

Slammed against metal
While tumbling head over heels
'Til I hit the ground

Harvest

The harvest began
Cattle driven to slaughter
They walked on two legs

All plucked from their homes
By mysterious forces
To hovering ships

Their captors unseen,
The people trembled in fear
They were abducted

Soon creatures appeared
And cut them down where they stood
While they tried to run

Huge black containers
Were filled with the dead bodies
By robotic claws

The containers rolled
To some type of space kitchen
For preparation

Not the first harvest
Mars came before us humans
With more planets left

We all suit their tastes
Billions and billions are served
We are the pink slime

Birds crowded the ledge
Jostling to see their victim
As she stepped outside

Father Patrick

We found Father Pat
And pulled him from the river
It wasn't pretty

Cinderblock anklets
And arms severed at the wrist
No tongue in his mouth

It was a message
They won't suffer a squealer
Not even a priest

Take all the bad ones
And skin all of them alive
Then coat them in salt

Quarantine

I don't believe that
My clean suit had a pinhole
It was sabotage

I know their methods
How they get their test subjects
With these "accidents"

Who would believe me?
They'd say I knew all the risks
That I was reckless

Locked in quarantine
They watch each new symptom start
Enjoying my pain

I'm just a number
Just a guinea pig or rat
No longer human

Acid burns her throat
Eating away her tissue
She can't even scream

Summers Past

Picking mulberries
Standing on a fallen limb
To reach the ripe fruit

Lazy summer day
Calluses on my bare feet
Promises of tarts

And hundreds of ants
Swarming angry to my knees
Fight or flight kicks in

I jump from the limb
And sprint down the gravel road
Wishing I'd worn shoes

Safe at home, breathless
My last time I picked berries
And ate those sweet tarts

In the end, we rot
There's no great secret to tell
Don't waste one moment

Acknowledgements

First, thank you for picking up and reading this book. Without readers, we writers really have no purpose. So, thank you!

A fancy thank you to the lovely and talented Jill Hejl for reading my poems and creating a cover that crawled right out of my brain.

Thank you to my beta readers for providing honest feedback. It was a joy to work with you all!

Thanks for the friendship and support from my good friends over at The Twisted Library Forum—I've never "met" a better group of people. (living or undead)

Most importantly, I need to thank my husband for listening to my stories and poems and being scared in the appropriate places. You give me the guts to do this and for that, I'm eternally grateful.

Carey Burns has been called weird on more than one occasion and is okay with it. When she isn't waxing poetic she is busy writing dark fiction or making jewelry. You can find her short stories in the following anthologies: <u>Through the Eyes of the Undead</u>, <u>Horrorology</u>, <u>The Zombist</u>, <u>Letters from the Dead</u>, <u>The Scroll of Anubis</u>, <u>Alienology: Tales from the Void</u>, <u>Zombidays</u>, and <u>Baconology</u>. Her poetry appears in <u>Putried Poetry and Sickening Sketches</u> and <u>Collabthology: Kindle of the Dead</u>. You can follow her on Twitter @justcareyburns or stop by her blog careyburns.blogspot.com.

Jill Hejl is an illustrator and artist who loves to use color and the humorous skewering of everyday life as her inspiration. She has always been drawn to Outsider art and children's artwork, both of which embody the lack of pretense and immediacy of emotion she strives for in her own work. Jill loves foreign languages, guitar jams, films, guacamole, lettering, books, paper products, quirky people, and hot tea on a rainy day.

Ms. Hejl lives with her husband and her animal children near Chicago. You can reach her at jillhejl@comcast.net.